MY MAMA SAYS

THERE AREN'T ANY

ZOMBIES, GHOSTS, VAMPIRES,

CREATURES, DEMONS, MONSTERS,

FIENDS, GOBLINS, OR THINGS

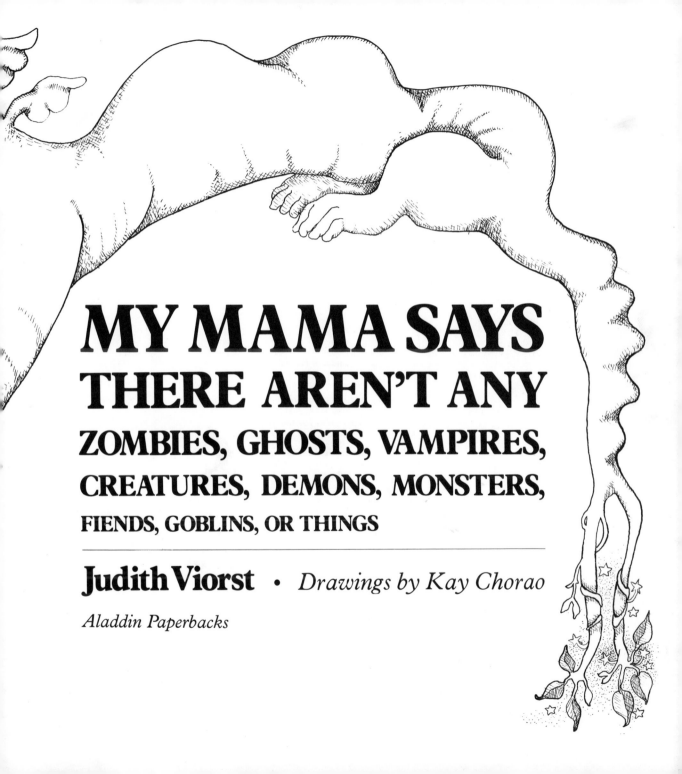

MY MAMA SAYS
THERE AREN'T ANY
ZOMBIES, GHOSTS, VAMPIRES,
CREATURES, DEMONS, MONSTERS,
FIENDS, GOBLINS, OR THINGS

Judith Viorst · *Drawings by Kay Chorao*

Aladdin Paperbacks

Aladdin Paperbacks
An imprint of Simon & Schuster
Children's Publishing Division
1230 Avenue of the Americas
New York, NY 10020

First Aladdin Paperbacks edition, 1977
Second Aladdin Paperbacks edition, 1988
Also available in a hardcover edition from Atheneum Books for Young Readers

Printed in Hong Kong

20   19

Library of Congress Cataloging-in-Publication Data
Viorst, Judith.
My mama says there aren't any zombies, ghosts, vampires, creatures,
demons, monsters, fiends, goblins, or things.
Summary: If his mother has made other important
mistakes, can Nick trust her word that there are no
goblins and such lurking around in the night?
[1. Mothers—Fiction. 2. Monsters—Fiction]
I. Chorao, Kay, ill. II. Title.
PZ7.V816My 1988 [E] 87-18733
ISBN 0-689-71204-9

To my very own Nick,
who helped me write this book.

My mama says there isn't any mean-eyed monster
with long slimy hair and pointy claws
going scritchy-scratch, scritchy-scritchy-scratch
outside my window.

But yesterday my mama said

I couldn't have some cream cheese on my sandwich,

because, she said, there wasn't any more.

And then I found the cream cheese

under the lettuce

in back of the Jello. So...

sometimes even mamas make mistakes.

My mama says that a vampire
isn't flying over my house
with his red and black vampire cape
and his vampire f-f-f-fangs.

But how can I believe her

when she said my wriggly tooth would fall out Thursday,

and then it stayed till Sunday after lunch?

And once she gave me 19 cents

when yo-yos cost a quarter. So...

sometimes even mamas make mistakes.

On certain nights
when everyone's cozy and sleeping,
all of a sudden I hear a Thing in the yard.
And you know what it says as it ooooozes along?
It says, Nick, I am coming to get you.
My mama says it's positively not.

But when we shopped at the supermarket Friday,
my mama told me to carry the bag with the eggs.
It's heavy, I said, too heavy for me.
Oh, you can do it, she told me.

I can't.

You can.

I can't.

You can.

I can't.

You can, she told me.

And that's how there got to be scrambled eggs
all over my shoes.

And that lady. So...

sometimes even mamas make mistakes.

And sometimes in my bunk bed I start thinking,

maybe a fiend sneaked into my lower bunk.

And he's sniffing around for a boy to eat,

and I'm the boy that he's sniffing, and…

My mama says no fiends have sneaked in here.

But why did she scold me for leaving my skates
on the sidewalk?
Those were Anthony's skates.
I remembered to put mine away.

And once she said I hadn't flushed,

and it was Alexander's. So...

sometimes even mamas make mistakes.

My mama says that a tall white ghost
who goes "hoo!" from a hole in its mouth,
isn't hoo-hoo-hooing in my closet.

This morning, though, she made me wear my boots.

And then it didn't rain—or even drizzle.

And once I asked for chocolate nut
and she brought back rum raisin. So…
sometimes even mamas make mistakes.

My mama says that a zombi

with his eyes rolled back in his head,

and his arms out stiff,

and his skin as cold as ice,

isn't clonking up and up the stairs.

But how can I believe her

when she told me Holly's middle name was Susan.

And Holly's middle name is really Jane.

And once she said I wasn't
when I told her I was going to be car sick. So...
sometimes even mamas make mistakes.

And sometimes in the dark a demon

is switching his spidery tail.

And waiting.

Waiting for someone.

Who could it be?

And he's laughing a "heh!"

And a "hah!"

And a "hee!"

Which could give someone goose bumps in summer.

He isn't there, my mama says to me.

But how does she know

when she still doesn't know how to drive me

to Christopher's house without getting us lost on the way?

She tells me, Zip your jacket up.

But she can't zip it either. So…

sometimes even mamas make mistakes.

And I'm sure I've seen a goblin
slinking out of my dresser drawer
with a sack on his back to take me to goblin-y lands
where boys and girls eat brussels sprouts
and never get a birthday.
Oh, no, you haven't, Mama always says.

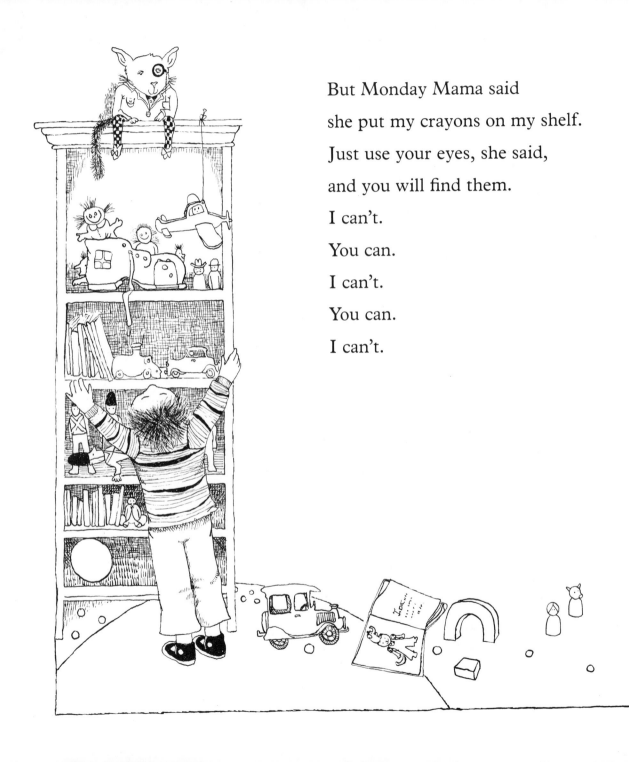

But Monday Mama said
she put my crayons on my shelf.
Just use your eyes, she said,
and you will find them.
I can't.
You can.
I can't.
You can.
I can't.

All right! *I'll* find them,
she said (not very nicely).
But, guess what?
She couldn't, too. So…
sometimes even mamas make mistakes.

My mama says that a creature
isn't reaching out his hand
to pinch me,
or squinch me,
or push me,
or squush me,
or—agggh!

Well, sometimes even mamas make mistakes.

But sometimes they don't.

Judith Viorst has been writing for the more than ten years that she has been married, with a lot of helpful encouragement from her husband and three sons. She loves children's books and tries to write books that her own children will like—and in which they will sometimes recognize themselves. Her husband is also a free-lance writer, and he works at home as she does. As one of their children once explained, "My father is a typewriter, and I think my mother is too." Among her books for children are *The Tenth Good Thing About Barney* and *Alexander and the Terrible, Horrible, No Good, Very Bad Day.*

Kay Chorao lives in New York City with her husband, Ernesto, and their three sons, Jamie, Peter and Ian. She graduated from Wheaton College in Massachusetts and did graduate study at The Chelsea School of Art in London, England. She is the author-illustrator of *The Repair of Uncle Toe* and *A Magic Eye for Ida.*